Why Hippo Loves the Water

An African Tale

Retold by Andrea Florens

Illustrated by Claire Norden

Long, long ago in Africa, there lived a Hippopotamus. When she was young, she was dainty and slim and she lived happily amongst the other animals on the land.

But as she grew older, Hippo became greedy.
No longer content with eating just a few meals, she would eat
all day long. She ate all the bananas off the banana tree.
She gobbled all the mangoes that she could find.
She grazed on acres of grass. And with her long strong teeth,
she munched all the coconuts before any of the other
animals could get their fair share.

munch

munch

munch

The animals on the land became very unhappy with Hippo.
"You have eaten all the bananas!" cried Monkey.
"Not one mango left for us!" moaned the fruit bats and the birds.

"And you've eaten most of the grass!" howled Zebra. "We are getting **thinner** and you are getting **fatter!**" they complained. But Hippo did not care. She munched and she crunched and she **gobbled** and she **guzzled**.

Every day Hippo became fatter and fatter.
And the bigger she grew, the hungrier she became.
Searching for another tasty meal, she wandered down to the
river where she saw Crocodile and Eagle eating some fish.

Without hesitation, Hippo waded into the river, and with her enormous mouth wide open, she caught as many fish as she could and swallowed them with one large gulp. How happy she was to find another scrumptious source of food! But even better, how pleasantly cool and comfortable she felt in the water.

But Crocodile and Eagle were not happy at all!
They chased after Hippo, pecking and snapping at her
until she escaped onto dry land.

And for the next few days, Hippo stayed far from the river. Eating as much as she could possibly find. Growing larger and larger by the day, her skin stretching ever so thin over her rounded body. The hot African sun began to bother her more and more. And the fatter she became, the worse the heat felt.

She longed for that **comfortable** feeling
of the water surrounding her body.
She dreamt of a life spent **wallowing**
in the cool river, eating fish all day long.
But her **fear** of Crocodile and Eagle
kept her away.

But as the days grew longer and the summer heat grew more fierce, Hippo felt her tight, thin skin scorching under the sun. Until one sweltering day, she could bear it no longer.

She quietly approached the river and mustering up all her **courage**, she called out to Crocodile and Eagle.

"Please help me!" she wailed "I can no longer live on the dry land. The sun is burning me so terribly!" And so she **pleaded** with them to let her **share** their river with her.

And although Crocodile and Eagle were rather **fearsome** creatures, they felt sorry for this unhappy, rotund Hippo and began to discuss her request amongst themselves.

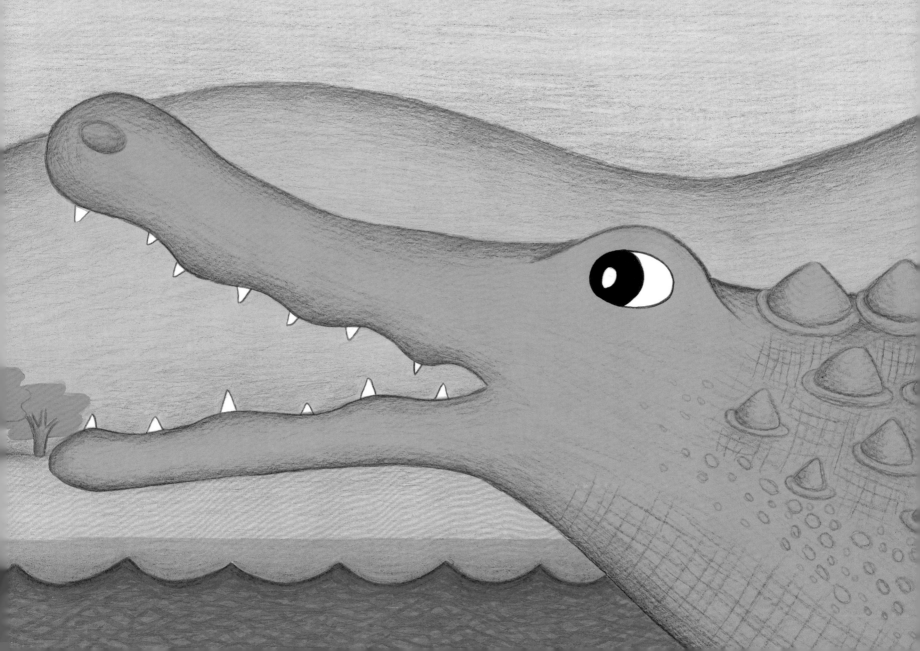

After much squabbling, Crocodile and Eagle returned
to Hippo with their decision.
"You may live in the water during the day to protect yourself
from the heat. But you are never allowed to eat
another fish ever again!" they said.

And with their beady eyes they gave a final **warning**, "We will always be **watching** you!"

Hippo made her **solemn** promise never to eat the fish again. And with that, she stepped into the **refreshing**, cool water. What **relief** she felt as she sank deeper and deeper, until only her eyes, ears and nostrils were visible.

To this day, Hippo spends her days wallowing
in the water, keeping herself protected from the burning sun.
At night she grazes on the grass, and once in a while she eats
fruit and nuts, making sure she's never too greedy.
And under the watchful eyes of Crocodile and Eagle, she spreads
her dung on the river bank, so they can be sure to find not one
fish bone, just as she promised.

Published in South Africa by Art Pub Printing (Pty) Ltd t/a Art Publishers
Reg. No 2018/329395/07
Unit BC3, 2 Linton Close, Beaconvale, Parow, Cape Town, 7500
Tel: +27 21 951 6391
www.artpub.co.za

Printed in South Africa by Shumani RSA in Parow, Cape Town

First Published 2020
Second revised edition 2022